The Villiage Crook
and Other Stories

Patricia Whittle

LMH PUBLISHING LIMITED

Editor: K. Sean Harris
Cover Illustration: Courtney Lloyd Robinson
Cover Design: Sanya Dockery
Book Design, Layout & Typesetting: Sanya Dockery

Published by LMH Publishing Limited
Suite 10-11, Sagicor Industrial Park
7 Norman Road
Kingston C.S.O., Jamaica
Tel.: (876) 938-0005; 938-0712
Fax: (876) 759-8752
Email: lmhbookpublishing@cwjamaica.com
Website: www.lmhpublishing.com

Printed in the U.S.A.   ISBN: 978-976-8245-54-0

NATIONAL LIBRARY OF JAMAICA CATALOGUING-IN-PUBLICATION DATA

Whittle, Patricia
    The village crook and other stories / Patricia Whittle.

    p. ; cm
ISBN 978-976-8245-54-0 (pbk)

1. Short stories, Jamaican   2. Jamaican fiction
I. Title

813   - dc 23

Dedication

I dedicate this book to my grandchildren,
Julian Kymario, Victora Xaria and Davia.

Contents

The Village Crook

Maas Fawni
and the Shopkeeper

In the cool hills of the Dry Harbour Mountains, in the district of Aboukir, lived a very crooked character. He was crooked in every sense of the word. He was lanky and lean, and he was dishonest. His name was Maas Fawni.

Maas Fawni lived alone in a one-room house that he rented. He was always well-dressed and clean. Everybody in the district knew him, but few people knew of his dishonest ways. He was a Jack of all trades and a master of none. Nobody knew exactly what work he did.

One day Mama sent Betty to the shop. "Come here, Betty," she called. "Run to the shop and buy some flour for me. The pot is on the fire already."

Betty took the fifty-dollar bill and ran toward the shop. On her way, she met Maas Fawni.

"Good morning, Maas Fawni," Betty said as she passed him.

"Morning, Betty," he replied. "Where are you going in such a hurry? Mind car hit yuh!"

Betty laughed. "I always walk on the right side of the road, Sir. Mama warned me to be careful."

"Good girl," Maas Fawni said. "I know you are smart. How much money yuh have in yuh hand?"

"Fifty dollars," answered Betty.

"Are you sure?" asked Maas Fawni. "Let me see it."

Now Betty was not so smart, for she gave the fifty dollars to him and when she was not looking, he marked an X on the bill.

"You are really smart," he flattered her. "It is fifty dollars, all right. Hurry up and get the goods for your mother."

Betty hurried to the shop and purchased the flour for her mother. She gave the money to Miss Icy, the shopkeeper, collected her change, and headed home. Mama was pleased that she came back so quickly.

As soon as Betty left the shop, Maas Fawni entered and headed straight for the counter.

"Good morning, Miss Icy," he greeted the shopkeeper.

"Good morning, Maas Fawni," she replied.

Maas Fawni wasted no time. "Sell me a pound of rice and a tin of sardine," he said.

Miss Icy weighed the rice in a plastic bag and rested it on the counter. She then took a tin of sardine from the shelf and handed both items to Maas Fawni. While Miss Icy worked, Maas Fawni engaged her in conversation.

"Then, Miss Icy, what a way the crime rate high! Yuh listen to the news this morning? I don't know what this world coming to."

"Times really getting serious," Miss Icy responded. "Too many people out of work, and the devil find work for idle hands." As she talked she gave the goods to Maas Fawni, then held out her hand to collect the money. "That will be forty-five dollars," she told him.

"A pay yuh already," Maas Fawni told her with an innocent smile on his face.

"No, I did not get any money from you," Miss Icy said. "I might be getting old, but my head is not taking water. Look in your pocket and see if the money is still there. The rice and the sardine cost forty-five dollars."

Maas Fawni became very angry. He was quite an actor. "Please for my change!" he demanded. "Money does not grow on trees. I gave you fifty dollars, so I want my five dollars change."

Other customers were now in the shop, waiting for the misunderstanding to be settled so they could be served. They had no idea who was telling the truth.

Maas Fawni singled out Maas Tom and started telling him his side of the story. "Is the last fifty dollar a have in mi name a give to this woman," he explained to Maas Tom.

"Don't call me woman!" said Miss Icy. "I have a name."

Maas Fawni ignored her and continued to acquaint Maas Tom with his problem. "I even draw X in the middle of the fifty-dollar bill a gave to her."

"Liar!" shouted Miss Icy. "You gave me no money!"

"Look inside yuh till, see if yuh don't find the fifty dollar a just give to yuh," advised Maas Fawni. "I mark X in the middle of it."

"Yes, Miss Icy, just look, for we want serve," pleaded Miss Mary, one of the customers.

Miss Icy opened the till and took out two fifty-dollar notes. She examined them and a puzzled look crept over her face. Just as Maas Fawni had said, there was an X in the middle of one of the notes.

Maas Fawni looked relieved. "I told you I gave you the money," he said. "Maybe yuh had something on yuh mind, Miss Icy. It sometimes happens to the best of us."

With that he collected his change, leaving Miss Icy very puzzled and quite disgruntled.

As Maas Fawni hurried home with the goods he had dishonestly acquired, he complimented himself on how smart he was. He had tricked Miss Icy, and everybody thought it was a genuine error on her part. He would go and cook his rice and sardine and plot his scheme for getting food another time.

Miss Icy, however, could not get the incident out of her mind. She was certain that Maas Fawni had given her no money. She wondered how the marked money had gotten inside the till. She decided that she would have to keep an eye on this man, Maas Fawni.

She would look out for him in the hope that he would be caught and punished if he kept on being dishonest.

Maas Fawni
Goes to Market

ave Valley market was noted for having an area where people sold animals such as cows, horses, mules, donkeys, goats and pigs. People from miles around would pass through Aboukir, leading their animals to sell at the market. Maas Fawni always bought his foodstuff at Cave Valley market. He carried two black scandal bags from his home, for he did not want to have to spend extra money to buy them at the market to put his goods into.

Maas Fawni walked all the way from Aboukir to Cave Valley, and he was quite thirsty. He was also tired and hungry. He did not have enough money to purchase a cooked meal, but the aroma from Miss May's restaurant was driving him crazy. He could hardly contain himself as he bought his vegetables and seasoning and the regular foodstuff to take him through the week. When that was done, Maas Fawni realized that he did not even have his bus fare to go home. He scratched his head as he contemplated walking home in the hot sun on his hungry belly.

All around him, people seemed to be quite content. He envied the fat higgler, who was helping herself to a plate of bammy and fried fish. He had to muster up all his resolve to prevent himself from begging Lisa for some of her curried goat. If he did, he knew he would never hear the end of it, for Lisa would just go about and spread lies on him. Instead, he asked Lisa about the goods she was selling.

"How much per dozen for those nice ripe bananas?" he asked, although he had no intention of buying any.

Lisa read his mind like a book, and she gave him a mean look. "Is forty dollars a dozen for them an' a beg yuh, no bother feel them up. Last week yuh feel up feel up mi nice tomatoes an' soften some a them an' walk away without even buying one. So if a buy yuh a buy, buy an' galang, but no touch nothing fi mi."

Maas Fawni moved away from her stall and bought two stringy mangoes with the little change he had in his pocket. He washed them at the standpipe and ate them quickly, but they only made him hungrier.

Before he knew it, he was inside Miss May's restaurant, boldly ordering a plate of rice and peas and fried chicken.

"What yuh want to wash it down with?" Miss May asked.

"Give mi a cream soda," Maas Fawni replied. He really loved that flavour, and he always boasted that it made him belch. "There is nothing that can take the gas off your stomach like a bottle a cream soda," he would say.

Maas Fawni quickly devoured the meal, but made sure to leave a little piece of meat and a few grains of rice on his plate. He then looked around carefully to make sure that no one was observing him. He reached inside his pocket and took out a dead cockroach and mixed it with the rice on his plate. That done, he beckoned to Miss May.

Miss May came at once to clear the table and collect the money for the meal, but instead of paying her, Maas Fawni showed her the dead roach in the food. "How can you be so careless?" he reprimanded her. "I have a mind to report this place to the public health inspector!"

Miss May's eyes widened in alarm. She still had two big pots of rice and a big pot of meat in the kitchen. Miss May could not afford to lose any of her customers, and this was what Maas Fawni was banking on.

"Never mind," Miss May said in a whisper. "I will bring you another lunch."

As she quickly collected his plate, Maas Fawni glared at her. "Don't bring me anymore if I have to pay for it," he said.

"Is all right," said Miss May. She felt that if she sweetened him up, he would forget about the whole incident.

As Maas Fawni devoured another plate of food, he congratulated himself on outwitting Miss May. He cleaned his plate, made a big belch and left the restaurant. It was all right for him to walk home now, for his belly was full with Miss May's delicious food.

Maas Fawni
Acts in a Play

Everybody was excited. There was going to be a big concert in the district of Aboukir. Every evening the participants could be seen rehearsing their parts. There was going to be traditional dancing, reciting of poems, singing of folk songs, and a play. It seemed as though the whole village was taking part.

Everywhere you went, people were talking about the big concert. It was to raise funds to help to build a community centre. Rehearsals took place in the old school building.

"Then Maas Fawni, yuh not taking part in the concert?" Miss Mirrie asked him.

"Of course a participating!" he proudly answered. "I am an actor in the play."

"Go deh, Maas Fawni!" encouraged Alvin. "Imagine Maas Fawni going star inna play!"

The fact was that Maas Fawni had only a small part in the play, but he loved to appear important. In the play, Maas Tom was supposed to call out "Matches! Matches!" to which Maas Fawni would reply, "No thank you." Maas Fawni should then take up his hat and leave the stage.

The big day of the concert came at last. Old and young did their part and everyone performed well. That is, everyone except Maas Fawni. When the time came for Maas Fawni to perform the little part he had, he was so nervous that everything before him was a blur.

"Matches! Matches!" shouted Maas Tom.

Maas Fawni said, "No thank you, and I take up my hat and I walk right out." In his fright, Maas Fawni forgot to leave the stage, and shouted the stage directions instead.

The audience went wild with laughter. Maas Fawni felt he was so good that they were cheering him. He stood on the stage, basking in the applause, and throwing the other actors into a state of confusion.

At the end of the concert, the director reprimanded him soundly for shouting out his stage directions instead of acting them, and for failing to leave the stage.

Maas Fawni
Stays at a Guest House

At dinner time, Maas Fawni consumed all the food, belched loudly, and announced, "A ketch three!" He was actually referring to the three meals he had eaten, but they were convinced that he was on to them.

The Windsor Guest House looked dilapidated and rundown, but it was never out of guests. This was because the food was good and many workers who travelled from afar to toil in the pepper factory found the cost to lodge at the Windsor quite reasonable.

The employees worked hard and treated the guests well, but among them were three dishonest waitresses named Dorothy, Adina and Eunice. They often borrowed money from the funds and conveniently forgot to replace it. The manager, an easygoing man, failed to notice that three of his trusted employees were robbing him blind.

Now, Maas Fawni, the seasoned 'ginnal', the Caribbean term for con man, came into the area to try out his luck with his trade, 'ginnalism'.

He lived from day to day by outwitting people, and he badly needed food and lodging. However, he did not have enough money to spend on such luxuries. He let the proprietors believe that he had just been hired at the factory, and needed an advancement of lodging until he got paid. If he got through, he intended to eat, sleep and disappear.

Mustering up his courage, he made his way to the check-in counter and requested a room for the night. He made sure to announce that he was a 'science man' and could read up people by just looking at them. On hearing this, the three crooked waitresses became very uneasy, and Maas Fawni immediately sensed their discomfort.

He put on his sly look and eyed them intently. After listening to his request, the manager was kind enough to give him a room until he got his first week's pay. Little did he know that Maas Fawni planned to abscond on the following day.

Maas Fawni slept well, for he was tired. In the morning he wasted no time in reaching the dining room, where he devoured the delicious breakfast of liver and fried dumplings, which Dorothy served him. He washed everything down with a tall glass of orange juice, belched loudly and announced, "A ketch one!"

Goodness! He knows that I have been robbing the boss, Dorothy thought to herself. She quickly found her accomplices and expressed her fear to them. Maas Fawni watched them keenly. He decided to tarry a little longer and see how things panned out.

Lunch time came, and bestowed upon Maas Fawni a big plate of rice and peas with peppered steak, served to him by Adina. He wiped it off in no time, followed it up with a large glass of ginger beer, belched loudly and said, "A ketch two!"

On hearing this, Adina was beside herself with fear. She was convinced that the 'science man' was on to her, too. She made her way over to the other two and delved into a deep conversation. Maas Fawni continued to watch them keenly. He realized that something was definitely amiss, so he decided to stay a little longer and check it out.

At dinner time, Eunice served him his dinner of plain rice and curried goat. He waxed it off, gulped down a glass of cream soda, belched loudly and announced, "A ketch three!" This was too much for the three thieves. Together they called Maas Fawni aside and begged him not to tell the boss about their dishonesty.

Maas Fawni was a smart one. Without saying a word, he listened and learned of their wrongdoings.

"If you keep our secret, you can stay for the rest of the week free," they offered.

He could hardly believe that luck could just drop in his lap like this, but experience taught Maas Fawni not to push his good fortune. Putting on a stern face, he reprimanded them for their dishonesty.

"I have a good mind to report you to the owner," he said. "I want nothing to do with you and your dishonesty. When I stay for the rest of the week free, as you put it, who will pay my bill?"

"We will," they answered in unison.

"I will just pack my things tomorrow morning and move on," he told them. "Pay the bill for my brief stay here."

Maas Fawni
and Mama Joyce

Once, when nobody had seen Maas Fawni for a few days, he returned with a big bag of mangoes and told people that he went to Clarendon, and that they treated him nice up there. After that he started making regular trips to Clarendon, and each time he returned with a lot of mangoes. Then one day he came back as pleased as puss, and everyone immediately knew that something was afoot.

Maas Fawni buys three pounds of beef from Uncle Dobson! Maas Fawni, who always buys sardine and rice, suddenly has money to buy beef! Maas Fawni buys new clothes! And the tongues wagged.

"A wonder which fool him con now?" Maas Tom wondered aloud.

But not a word did Maas Fawni utter about his good fortune. Everybody was guessing and spelling, until at last the story came out.

When Maas Fawni went to Clarendon he met an elderly woman named Mama Joyce. Her grandson, who was a lawyer, with his business place in Kingston, was there. They said the man was very handsome.

He came to spend the weekend with Mama Joyce, who was quite proud of him. The people complained that their ears couldn't 'eat grass' the way Mama Joyce praised up the young man. Maas Fawni met him also.

The story had it that the fellow confided in his grandmother, and told her how his business wasn't doing well at all. He and his batch mate from university set up the business in New Kingston.

"Granny mi graduate with first-class honours and mi business partner have upper-class honours, so I don't know what the problem is," he told her. "Other lawyers in the same complex are doing good business."

Mama Joyce told Maas Fawni about the problem and he, of course, persuaded her that he was just the man to solve the problem, since he was a man of science. He gave her some cock-and-bull story that her grandson had an enemy watching him and didn't want him to prosper.

Mama Joyce swallowed everything, hook, line and sinker.

Maas Fawni said to Mama Joyce, "Whatever a tell yuh now, must be in strict confidence. Nobody must know that a working for yuh, or the spell they put on the fellow will never break."

"Then what about mi grandson? Don't mi will have to tell him?" she asked.

"No!" warned Maas Fawni. "Find some way to force him to carry out the instructions that a going to give yuh, but yuh mustn't mention our little business at all."

"It sound serious like is big obeah them set pon mi grandson, after him father spend so much money pon him."

"Yes, but jus' be careful to follow mi instructions, then stand back an' witness the miracle."

Mama Joyce looked doubtful, and Maas Fawni detected it.

"I'm an honest man, but I see doubt in yuh eyes," he said. "I'm not going to take a penny from yuh until yuh see the good results. All I want today is my bus fare an' a little lunch. At the end of the month, after yuh grandson do what him mus do an' reap good results, then yuh pay mi. But remember, not a word to a soul."

"Mi lips are sealed," she told Maas Fawni. "How much it will cost?"

"Three pounds," said Maas Fawni, without blinking an eye.

"All right."

"Yuh grandson has to remove his name from the sign on the door of his office. Let him put the name of his business partner on the door instead. By the way, what is the name of the partner?"

"Mr. Harry Virtue."

"Well the sign must now read Harry Virtue & Associate, Attorneys at Law."

Mama Joyce followed the instructions to the letter, and the business picked up like wildfire. They got so many clients that people had to start making appointments to see them. Mama Joyce was so elated; she didn't even wait for the month to end. She sent for Maas Fawni and paid him the fee with a bonus.

Maas Fawni pocketed the cash and went home to bask in his new-found wealth.

"Let them wonder," he told Maas Jimmy. "I have to think on mi feet to earn my living. Is gullible people like those put bread on my table. But yuh know, Jimmy, what I can't understand is how an intelligent educator could expect him son to succeed in the lawyer business when him write him name so big an' bold on him office door."

"But nothing nuh wrong with that," Jimmy interrupted. "That's what all lawyers do."

"But him father is a professor at the university. He should be smarter than that!"

"Yuh confusing me," Jimmy said.

"But what in God's name, mek Professor John Swindler an' him wife call the poor boy Adam?"

Maas Fawni's
Luck Runs Out

Maas Alex was losing his cows. Somebody was cutting off the cows' tails and the culprit was very elusive. Some people swore that the thief was a woman. Others claimed that it was a very evil duppy that a certain woman set on Maas Alex, because he had robbed a lot of money from her. The tongues kept wagging, but the culprit kept escaping.

"Yuh don't catch the thief yet, Maas Alex?" people would ask him.

His answer was always the same. "When I lay hand on that crook, a going chop him up as sure as my name is Robert Alexander Bush!"

The truth was that Maas Alex was really under pressure. He lived in a big house on a farm. Maas Alex was black and muscular, and was usually dressed in a khaki shirt and pants, and black water boots.

His wife was slim and brown with long black hair, which she wore in a bun. She was a teacher at the Eccleston Primary School. While other children walked around barefooted, their two children wore socks and shoes everywhere they went, and always had money for ice cream and chocolate. To cut a long story short, they were rich.

So people couldn't understand why he made such a fuss when children raided his guava trees or the mango trees and apple trees. They said he preferred to let the fruits drop and waste on the ground rather than give them away. Maybe that was why certain people started helping themselves to things on his farm. He was angry about the theft of the fruits and farm produce, but he was like a raging bull when it came to the loss of his cows.

Within two months he had lost three of his cows. The severed tail of his bull got badly infected, and the animal became very sick and eventually died. As if that was not enough, another day he woke up to find his prize heifer that had just given birth, tail-less. The thief had cut off the whole tail. Maas Alex did all that he could to save the cow, but it lost so much blood that it too eventually died. The calf was too young to fend for itself, so it also died.

People really did not like Maas Alex very much. They found him to be mean and exact. If he lent them money, he charged them too much interest. He charged them too much for milk from the cows. Alvin, who worked for him on the farm, complained how he was instructed to dump the excess milk instead of giving it to people who needed it. But in spite of all this, the people despised the thief who robbed the cows of their tails, and in solidarity, they vowed to catch the culprit.

Since nobody knew for sure who the thief was, they had to be very careful. Maas Alex bought six fierce dogs and hired men from a security firm to guard his farm. After that, the thefts stopped.

A month went by, then two, then three, and nothing else was stolen. Who would dare to face the angry dogs or the security guards? Maas Alex was taking no chances.

But soon other people complained of losing things from their farms. Now many of these farms were at the back of people's houses, because in their homes, these country people had big land space on which they cultivated cash crops.

Maas Ernest got up one morning only to discover that someone had cut his big bunch of bananas during the night. A few weeks after that, someone dug up a whole yam hill of Maas Arthur's yam. Little by little, the thief was helping himself, or herself, to people's crops.

Just as everybody was losing their patience, someone spotted the thief. Early one morning, he glimpsed the culprit and cried, "Thief! Thief!"

The cry came from Maas Sam. Maas Sam had his little cultivation to the side of his house. He planted yam, potatoes, peas and corn. He also had two donkeys which pulled his cart from which he sold his farm produce. He would pass through the district on Saturdays yelling, "Buy sweet yellow yam from yuh food man, Sam! A have potatoes as big as yuh head. Who no wan' potato, buy peas an' corn instead!"

The people were amused at the way Maas Sam advertised his goods. He had a cow, which he kept tied to the orange tree. He hoped to fatten the cow with a lot of grass and then sell it to Maas Dan, the butcher, at a good price.

It was still dark, so when the people ran out, they could hardly see anything. "Where is the dirty thief?" they demanded. "If we catch him, him done fah!"

With that they started searching the yard, but saw no sign of a thief. Suddenly Bob, Maas Sam's son, shouted, "See a strange woman running from behind the wall!"

Sure enough, someone had dashed into the bushes behind the wall, but by the time the crowd had descended on the bush, the person escaped.

The men gave chase, following the shadow, but when they reached Maas Fawni's house, they saw a woman's figure jump the fence and elude them again.

They ran through Maas Fawni's yard and knocked on his door. "Maas Fawni!" they shouted. "Wake up, man! Thief in yuh yard! Come help catch her!"

Maas Fawni had left his back window open, and was able to jump through it and close it just in the nick of time. Shortly after he had vaulted through and slammed the window shut, he heard them knocking down his door.

"Good Lord!" he shouted, although his lungs were bursting. "Can't a decent citizen get some rest? Let the young boys them chase thief. Them strong and hearty. Let a poor man get him rest!"

The people became angry that Maas Fawni was so lazy. "Is everybody business to catch the thief!" they shouted. "Mine is you hiding her? We see a woman run into yuh yard!"

"Open the door let we see for weself that she not hiding in there!" demanded Maas Sam.

"Are you crazy?" Maas Fawni asked.

But they would not leave and kept pounding on the door until Maas Fawni opened it.

"Look for oonuhself," he advised them. They looked and were satisfied that no one was hiding in Maas Fawni's house.

"All right," said Maas Sam, "but yuh is a lazy an' unhelpful man. Yuh time will come one day an' a hope no one will lift a hand to help yuh. Galang back go sleep an' snore!"

"Thank you very much," Maas Fawni retorted as he reached to close the door.

Just then Maas Sam spotted something. A grayish lock of hair was covered under a dish cloth on the table. Maas Sam pushed Maas Fawni aside and lifted the cloth. His mouth dropped in amazement. Curled up under the dish cloth was the tail of one of his donkeys.

"Everybody come back here!" shouted Maas Sam. "At last we catch the thief! See the evidence on the table here!"

Maas Fawni opened his mouth to protest, but he couldn't get out of this one. The crowd came down and beat the daylight out of him. It was Maas Sam same one who had to rescue the crook.

"We have to tek bad things mek laugh!" jeered Maas Egbert. "Yuh mean time so hard wid him, that him start eat donkey tail!"

"Is mi cow him was after, but in the dark him mek mistake an' cut off the donkey tail instead!" Maas Sam said angrily.

They searched the house again and found a wig and some dresses. All these they collected as evidence that Maas Fawni was the elusive crook.

They reported him to the police, and he was dragged off to jail.

What was left of the donkey's tail was dressed and cared for, and luckily the donkey survived, for Maas Sam really could not afford to buy another donkey.

As for the dishonest Maas Fawni, he spent a long time in jail. No one called him Maas Fawni again. He won the name Maas Donkey Tail.

When he was released from jail, he did not return to Aboukir. He was too ashamed to go back. So if you ever see a lean and lanky man asking children to show him their money, don't let them show him. If you see a lean and lanky man putting a roach in his food at a restaurant, don't let him get away with it. It might just be Maas Donkey Tail, previously known as Maas Fawni.

The Story
Of
Maas Tom

Maas Tom

The village of Clackton was noted for its fertile soil and green pastures. Most of the villagers did farming for a living, but there were also a few teachers, nurses, a post mistress, a public health inspector, police officers and carpenters.

Tom Mason was a resident in the village. Everybody knew him as Maas Tom. People described him as a handsome black man. He was tall and muscular, and whenever he laughed, he opened his mouth wide, displaying strong white teeth. He had a big appetite and he loved to cook and take the lion's share.

Maas Tom was a farmer. He lived with his family on a big farm, where he reared cows, goats, pigs and chickens. He also cultivated yams, potatoes and other farm produce which he supplied to higglers and other business people. Every Friday a van would come to purchase goods from the farm.

Maas Tom's family consisted of his wife, Edna, and five children. There were three girls and two boys, ranging from age six to twelve. The boys were Milton and Robert, aged eight and ten respectively. The girls were Pamella, six, Candy, nine, and Peggy, twelve.

Now Maas Tom was a kind man. Some people felt that he was too kind for his own good.

He seldom missed a chance to help people who were in need and he was always kind to children. It was therefore very unfortunate that Maas Tom was illiterate. Edna was intelligent though. She helped Maas Tom to manage his business and gave him sound advice.

She believed strongly in putting away something for a rainy day, and she made sure that the children attended school regularly.

Maas Tom was a stubborn man, who usually ignored Edna's good advice. This often resulted in bad consequences. Maas Tom attended church regularly, and believed strongly that one should never spare the rod and spoil the child. The children could not form the fool when Maas Tom was around.

At school it was a different matter. The girls were well behaved and they were also brilliant, but Robert and Milton were quite mischievous. They never seemed to be able to settle down in class and they often ignored their homework.

Robert was a student in Miss Stern's class. Miss Stern started each day with a story which the class always looked forward to hearing. As her name suggested, she was also a stern teacher. On her desk, she kept a thick ruler which she often used to beat students. Good students had nothing to fear from her, but those who misbehaved or failed to do good work would be clouted with constant claps from Miss Stern's thick ruler.

It was Thursday, a sunny day. Miss Stern told the class a lovely story about a boy whose father gave him a coat of many colours. Robert sat entranced as he listened to the fantastic story.

He enjoyed it from beginning to end. He wished his father would give him something nice for his birthday, which was coming up shortly. He was tired of getting gifts of handkerchiefs and caps.

"Now," said Miss Stern, "story time is over. It's time for some serious work. Today, I am going to test you on the words you studied for homework."

She opened her register and as she called each name, the student had to spell a word given by the teacher. Those who were unable to spell the word remained standing.

"Betty Brown, spell milk!"

"Sydney Evans, spell goat!"

"Carol Gordon, spell grass!"

One by one the children stood and spelt a word. Robert hoped that when his time came around he would spell his word correctly. Then, he started daydreaming about the beautiful coat. Maybe he would ask for a beautiful shirt, one with lions on it, or a T-shirt with a picture of Bob Marley, or a sweater with... Robert was so deep in thought that he did not hear Miss Stern call his name.

"Robert Mason spell cow!" she shouted for the third time. As Robert jumped up, he knocked over his chair and the class laughed.

"What sweet oonuh?" Robert asked loudly, ignoring the teacher's command.

Miss Stern was angry that the boy found time to be rude instead of spelling the word given to him.

"Come here this minute, Robert!" she demanded. "Open your hand!"

Robert was afraid of beatings. Each time the ruler descended, he pulled back his hand. A few of the blows connected, and unfortunately, the ruler caught his index finger and sprained it. After a time it became black and blue, and swollen. Miss Stern was not aware that Robert's finger was injured because the boy did not bring it to her attention. The rest of the day went well, and after they said their evening prayer, she reminded the children to go straight home and not idle on the road.

The following morning, Miss Stern marked the register and noted that Robert was absent. She thought nothing of it. She taught her class as usual and was about to send the children out for a short morning break, when she saw Robert and his father coming towards her classroom.

Robert was not in his uniform so she wondered what was wrong.

"Please come in," she said, as Maas Tom knocked on the door of the classroom.

"Good morning Mr. Mason," she greeted him. "What has Robert done now?"

"Morning Teacher," Maas Tom replied as he pushed Robert forward. "I is here because yuh beat Robert yesterday an' sprain him finger."

"But I was not aware that I sprained his finger," she said, surprised. "I am so sorry."

"The boy say that him nuh do anything an' yuh beat him," said Maas Tom.

"That's not so," said Miss Stern. "I told Robert to spell a very simple word, cow. Instead of spelling the word he found time to -"

Maas Tom did not wait for her to finish. "Good God Teacher!" he declared. "How yuh expect Robert to spell a big animal like cow? Why yuh didn't give him something small like mosquito to spell instead?"

"But Mr. Mason," said Miss Stern. "The size of the animal has nothing to do with the spelling of the word. It is all a matter of phonics."

Maas Tom was not listening. "I don't spoil the rod when pickney thief an' lie or fight!" he told her. "But yuh can't give the child this big everlasting animal to spell, an' then beat him on top of that! An' yuh mus' be careful how yuh beat children for see the boy finger swell up there!"

With that, he took Robert's hand and stomped through the door, leaving a very flustered Miss Stern, and a very amused class.

The Letter

Maas Tom's visit to Miss Stern's class spread like wildfire. Some of the students felt that Maas Tom was joking. They just could not believe that a big man could be so stupid. Others realized that he was very serious and did not know any better. It was a real source of embarrassment to Maas Tom's children.

The girls tried to ignore the remarks that other students made whenever they saw them. However, after a time they could take the taunting no more and many fights resulted. Miss Edna and Maas Tom heard about the fights and gave them strict orders not to fight at school again. They should practise self control, so they tried their best to ignore the unkind remarks of the students. Even if any of them got into a fight, they did everything to conceal it from their parents.

One day Peggy wrote a composition and it was so interesting that Miss Abby, her teacher, read it to the entire class. Peggy felt so good!

She would tell her mother the good news when she reached home; she would be so pleased!

On her way home from school, Adassa, the dullest girl in the class, started teasing her.

"How come you get so much for your composition an' yuh father can't read?" she asked.

Peggy ignored her and that angered Adassa. "Is who fa father nuh know B from bull foot?" she jeered.

At this Peggy lost her temper and lunged at her, using her long finger nails to scratch her face.

Surprised, Adassa grabbed her uniform and ripped a section of the skirt from the waist. Peggy held on to her uniform.

"Yuh see what yuh do!" she shouted at Adassa. Peggy was terrified. She knew that she would get a sound beating if her father found out that she was fighting.

As bad luck would have it, when Peggy reached home, her father was seated on the verandah.

She used her books to hide the torn dress, but Maas Tom sensed that something was wrong.

"Come here Peggy," he said. "Put your books here."

"I'll take them inside," said Peggy.

Maas Tom saw the torn clothes and the flushed face.

"What happen to yuh Peggy?" he demanded.

"A girl fight mi," said Peggy. She had to tell the truth, since she knew her father would hear about the fight from Candy or her brothers even if she lied.

"How much time mi an' yuh mother tell yuh not to fight at school!" shouted Maas Tom as he removed his belt and gave her a good beating. "Next time yuh fight a school a going to peel the red skin from yuh bottom!"

31

Miss Edna did not like when Maas Tom flogged the children. She rushed on to the verandah and pulled Peggy away.

"Why yuh go fight at school now?" she asked as she consoled her. When Peggy told her what caused the fight, Miss Edna became very angry with Maas Tom.

"Is you cause the child to fight at school!" she blamed him. "Imagine yuh didn't even ask Peggy why she fight before yuh go beat har! She would tell yuh that is Adassa teasing her 'bout how yuh can't read! Because of yuh, the children can't even go to school in peace. Tom why yuh don't put away yuh stubborn pride and learn to read? Look how many times a try to teach yuh. Look how many times mi advise yuh to go to JAMAL class!"

JAMAL was an acronym for Jamaica Movement for the Advancement of Literacy. In the seventies the government introduced the movement to help eradicate illiteracy. There were classes island-wide, where people could learn to read and write.

"Is yuh spoil the confounded pickney dem!" shouted Maas Tom. "A forbid them to fight and them fight, so them mus' feel. Yuh think otherwise, so they do as they like with yuh. With all the knowledge yuh have, yuh can't even control the pickney dem!" With that he took his bag and machete and stormed out of the house.

Shortly after Maas Tom left, Pamella and Candy came in. Candy, on seeing Peggy crying, asked what was the matter.

"No bother mi!" Peggy shouted at her.

"Oh a beating yuh get," opined Candy. "Serve yuh right. Is you cause me to get a beating last time sake a chat-chat!"

Peggy made a face at her.

"Yuh ugly like duppy," Candy jeered.

"Yuh better stop bother mi or I'll lick yuh down!" shouted Peggy.

"Do it nuh," challenged Candy. "Do it if yuh think yuh bad!"

Peggy doubled her fist and hit Candy in her eye.

"Mi eye blind! Mi eye blind!" she screamed as she jumped and stomped about.

Miss Edna came running in. "Look at the child who just get beating to fight!" she observed. "Peggy is blind yuh blind yuh sister eye now! Oonuh live like puss and dog! A bet if Tom was here this couldn't happen. What a going to tell him when him come home?"

"Candy you go and sweep the yard!" she commanded. "Devil find work give idle hands."

Shortly after that Maas Tom came back with a bunch of half ripe bananas. He rested it on the table and called Candy to give him some water.

"What happen to yuh eye Candy?" he asked, observing her swollen eye that was now black and blue.

Miss Edna quickly answered. "Is a accident, Tom," she said. "Shortly after yuh gone she— "

"Is not any accident!" Candy quickly piped in. "Is Peggy lick mi in mi eye!"

Maas Tom was furious. "Edna, how yuh in the house an' mek this happen?" he demanded. "A only hope yuh give Peggy a sound beating!"

"Yuh would really want mi to beat her again after how yuh batter her this evening?" she inquired of Maas Tom. "Yuh don't have to beat them every time they do anything wrong. Yuh can find other ways to punish them. In fact, the medical book say beating do more harm than good to children, so mi jus want yuh to know since yuh can't read it for yuhself."

"All dem foolishness a jus' theory," said Maas Tom. "Somebody with nothing to do write them. By the way, where Robert and Milton now?"

"They gone to search for pears," she told him.

"Go for them. A don't like when they go on the farm too late," he said.

As soon as Edna left, Maas Tom called Candy. "Come here to mi Candy."

Candy thought he was going to beat her. "Is not me start the fight," she told him.

"I don't want to hear anything else 'bout that till a see you an' Peggy together," he said. "Yuh can read good?"

"Yes Papa," she answered. "Sometimes teacher let me read to the class at school."

Maas Tom took a letter from his pocket and gave her. "Read this to mi," he said.

As Candy was about to read the letter, Maas Tom hesitated. "Wait!" he demanded. "I don't want any pickney to know mi business." He placed Candy on a chair and used his two index fingers to cork up her ears. "Read now and don't try to listen what yuh reading!" he shouted.

It was very uncomfortable to have her ears corked up, but Candy read aloud.

Dear Tom,

I am sorry that I can't send the five hundred dollars that I borrow from you today, as I did promise you, I will try and let you get it on Friday. Don't worry yourself. I don't think Edna will miss it before I repay you. Thanks again. Gloria.

As soon as she finished reading the letter, Maas Tom took it from her and tore it up.

The Lollipop

Thursday turned out to be a bright and sunny day. Miss Edna sent the children to school and then busied herself with the housework. "When people are busy time really fly fast," she said to herself when the children returned in the evening. She was so busy with the housework that she did not even have time to cook.

Miss Edna told Pamella to hurry up and take off her uniform and run to the shop to buy some rice. She would give them rice and corned beef for dinner today. That would not take long to cook.

Pamella took the money and headed for the shop, which was close by. As she passed Candy she said, "I'm going to buy lollipop and yuh not getting any."

"Bring one fi mi man," begged Candy. They really loved lollipop, and each time they went to the shop, they would ask Miss Edna to let them buy lollipop with the change.

Robert and Milton were playing marbles and Peggy and Candy were doing their homework. Robert heard a funny gurgling noise and anxious footsteps approaching. He looked up to see poor Pamella drenched in sweat, holding her throat and choking to death.

"Run for Mama and Papa!" he shouted to Milton as he surveyed Pamella. Maas Tom and Miss Edna dashed from the house and soon realised that a lollipop was choking Pamella. "Run for a piece of bread!" she shouted at Maas Tom. He was so frightened that he ran back with the whole bread. Miss Edna quickly broke off a piece and pushed it into Pamella's mouth. "Swallow that," she said. "It will send down the lollipop."

The bread only made matters worse. Instead of dislodging the lollipop, it stuck in her throat alongside the lollipop.

"Run go call Maas Leelan!" she ordered Robert. "Tell him to bring him taxi right now. Tell him is a matter of life or death!"

Robert dashed off to get Maas Leelan who owned a taxi. By now a little crowd had gathered and everybody wanted to help, but nobody was successful so far.

"Maas Leelan is a hard man," said Maas Sam, one of the neighbours. "Him money come first or nothing doing."

"The money alright," Miss Edna said. "However, Maas Leelan could never be so hard to worry 'bout money at a time like this."

"You stay there," said Maas Sam. "He who feels it knows it."

Maas Leelan was a mean and stingy man. He always demanded his money before moving an inch with his taxi. He did not believe in credit. It was always 'pay as you enter'.

"Mama, Pamella going to die for there is no money in the house," said Candy, as she pulled at Miss Edna's dress.

Miss Edna ignored her as she anxiously observed Pamella who was still gulping and choking.

Milton, who had been pacing the area, not knowing what to do, suddenly grabbed Pamella and gave her a resounding blow in the back.

"Boy yuh gone stark staring mad!" shouted Maas Tom.

"Yuh want to kill yuh sister?" asked Miss Edna.

They let out a sigh of relief as the lollipop and bread flew out of Pamella's mouth as a result of the blow Milton gave her.

Everyone was relieved. Miss Edna now turned her attention to Candy.

"Candy how yuh mean to say that no money in the house? You're a child an' yuh mustn't chat what yuh don't know 'bout."

"But is true Mama," Candy assured her. "Papa lend Miss Gloria the five hundred dollars."

Miss Edna confronted Maas Tom. "Tom a true the child talking?" No answer.

"Tom you're a wicked man. Yuh take mi rainy day money an' lend it out. No wonder yuh stand there opening an' shutting yuh mouth like when frog inna quinsy! Imagine the child could dead an' —"

"But a how the pickney hear what was in the letter?" Maas Tom wondered aloud. "How she manage to hear when mi use mi own two finger an' cork up her ears when she was reading the letter?"

An explosion of laughter erupted from the crowd. Some rolled on the ground laughing. They could not believe their ears. Maas Leelan wondered if he was hearing or dreaming this and poor Miss Edna was so ashamed.

"Sometimes we have to take bad things mek laugh," she said as she carried Pamella inside.

Better Late Than Never

After the incident with the letter, Miss Edna felt so ashamed that she hardly went out again. She was so conscious of what people were saying behind her back, that she was afraid to face them. Maas Tom was not making it any easier for her either. He became very defensive whenever she came up with the subject of reading.

As for the children, they were jeered and harassed at school. They did not even want to go back to school, but Miss Edna would have none of that. She encouraged them to be strong and ignore the taunting and jeering, but they had to go to school.

There were some people in the community who wanted to help her though. They felt that Maas Tom was a good man, but he was really too stubborn. They knew that Miss Edna had been trying for a long time to get him to go to the JAMAL classes too.

Maas Leelan, Maas Sam and some other men came up with a plan. Maas Leelan was the one who told Miss Edna about it, and although she had her doubts, she welcomed the help.

Maas Tom loved to play dominoes. Maas Leelan kept inviting him to come and play dominoes with the domino posse. He told Maas Tom how exciting it was and how they were practising for a competition and wanted him on the team. The men played the game on Friday and Saturday nights. Maas Tom joined the players and enjoyed himself tremendously.

Later Mr. Jones, the teacher, joined them. He invited the men to stay back after each session of dominoes and help him with a project. All the men agreed, including Maas Tom.

Mr. Jones carried a bag which he opened after letting the men sit at the domino tables. He gave each man a book. It was a book with simple words along with the letters of the alphabet. Mr. Jones started by letting the men repeat the letters of the alphabet after him. Maas Tom was surprised to see all the men cooperating so he followed suit. Mr. Jones used the rest of the evening to go over the letters again and again. Maas Tom found himself enjoying the exercise. At the end of the class, Mr. Jones told them to keep the books and learn everything about the alphabet and the letter A on their own.

Maas Tom took the book home, but said nothing to Miss Edna. He found time to study the letters on his own. Miss Edna observed him, but she didn't say a word. When the weekend came around, Maas Tom went back to play dominoes and join the class afterwards.

Little by little he learnt the letters, then he learnt little words, then bigger words. The process was slow, and many times he felt like giving up, but Mr. Jones was cunning and so were the men. They always found ways to motivate Maas Tom and others like him to press on.

Maas Tom learned to sign his name and after two years he could read and write fluently. Miss Edna was so happy!

"It's better to be late than never," she said.

As for Maas Tom, he was still learning. He believed in perfection, and he wanted to write a book some day. He also motivated people to go to JAMAL classes. Sometimes he told them about his experiences. Whenever he spoke about the letter, they took it as a big joke.

"No one could be so stupid," they would often say.

Dudley
the Lunatic

The Chase

Was this a bad dream? Gloria had no time to pinch herself to find out. She was out of breath. She felt as if she would collapse any minute now. She was running for her life and a maniac was in swift pursuit.

For Gloria, Monday morning was no different from other work-days. She went through the same routine - she woke up at 6 a.m., got ready for work, then headed for the bus stop. But this morning as she bent the corner, a ragged creature armed with a machete sprang out at her.

She dropped everything she had and fled like lightning. As bad luck would have it, no one was around to rescue her. She kicked off her high-heeled shoes and sprinted across the playfield. She knew that Uncle Bob's house was just behind the playfield. She would holler for help and he would rescue her. Uncle Bob was an early riser.

Gloria heard the heavy footsteps close behind her. Her pursuer from hell was breathing heavily.

Help me Lord, she silently prayed.

Gloria's bad dream was Dudley. Dudley was once a handsome young man, tall and slim with eyes sharp and alert. After graduating from a prominent high school, he worked briefly as an accountant. He was admired by many girls in the village of Walden.

Gradually, however, conditions took a turn. His boss and co-workers were the first to notice it. Dudley's attitude was changing — for the worse.

He started coming to work late, and he was often absent. This had to be noticeable, since this was an employee who previously had never been late. To make matters worse, a few customers complained that he had been rude to them. This was so unlike the handsome, polite accountant who used to charm both customers and workers.

"You know I was considering him for a promotion," Mr. Denver, the manager, confided to Dudley's supervisor. "That young man needs counselling. I wonder what's his problem?"

What Mr. Denver didn't know, was that Dudley was taking drugs. It started off with a spliff.

"Only this once, only one try to see how it feels," he told himself. But after that he was hooked. He became a seasoned ganja smoker and a very carefree worker.

As if that was not bad enough, one of the dealers introduced him to cocaine. At first he was reluctant, but Bux, one of the vendors, urged him to just try it once. Dudley took a long sniff of the cocaine, and was instantly immersed into a sea of ecstatic bliss. When he came back to himself, he knew he had to try it again.

"This is better than an orgasm!" he blurted out.

Bux felt pleased. To him another customer, another addict, meant more cash.

So Dudley became Bux's customer. His little savings dwindled and so did his brain. Gradually he lost his friends, his job and his mind.

With no job and no money to support his addiction, Dudley began to steal. His family migrated, and the landlord evicted him from the house. He took refuge in a one-room house nearby and nobody bothered him, so he made it his home.

Now here was Dudley, armed with a machete, chasing poor Gloria, and for what? If he wanted money, he would have grabbed her handbag when she threw it at him. Poor Gloria! If Dudley chopped her up what would become of Dill and Valerie, her two children? Although she was now close to Uncle Bob's house, she did not have the strength to holler. She was at the mercy of this raving lunatic.

He caught up with her. She had no strength to go another inch. The stench of his stale breath and his sweaty clothes overwhelmed her. Cowering with fear, she closed her eyes and waited to die.

The machete went up, then it descended slowly, with a gentle tap on her bottom.

Gloria had heard horrendous stories of people being chopped to death. She tried not to think of the pain. She hoped it would be swift, but this wicked idiot seemed to want to prolong her pain.

Mustering what was left of her courage, she slowly opened her eyes to see her tormentor dashing across the playfield.

"Your time to catch me now!" he shouted.

My Uncle

Uncle Dudley was not always mad. He was my big uncle. Uncle Dudley used to work in an office. Every month end he would treat me and Janice to ice cream. He would also give us ten dollars to buy sweets. We loved our uncle.

We liked to play with him. Together we played lick and run, skip and sometimes he would give us 'donkey ride' on his back. Uncle Dudley could run fast. But after Uncle Dudley lost his job, he wasn't so nice again. He got angry with us for the least little thing, and he did not want to play with us anymore, and he moved from the big house to live into a little room. He slept and ate in the same room. He cooked outside and sat on his bed and ate his food.

Uncle Dudley did not have many visitors. Apart from me and Janice, only Miss Melda visited him. She tidied his room and cooked for him. When I asked Uncle Dudley if he could afford to pay her, he laughed. I did not see any joke, so I did not ask again.

After a time, Miss Melda moved into the little room with Uncle Dudley. When I asked Uncle Dudley where she slept, he just laughed, so I stopped asking questions. Miss Melda did not go out to work. She just stayed at home and washed or cooked outside. When Uncle Dudley was not at home, she walked about and gossiped with anyone who would listen to her.

She demanded money from Uncle Dudley, so he had to work hard to support her. He often went into the woods and cut trees. He then sold the lumber and the money supported them. I don't think he gave Miss Melda all the money, though. He kept enough to buy drugs and of late, he started to drink rum. People used to laugh and say, "Every hoe have dem stick a bush." Miss Melda was a good match for Uncle Dudley. I know Uncle Dudley loved her, but I often wondered if she cared one hoot about him. She would often tell people how simple he was and they gave jokes about him and laughed behind his back.

Uncle Dudley would often go deep into the woods and remain there for up to five days. He would cut a lot of lumber and a truck would come and pick them up for money.

On these occasions, Tony would come to the house. He even slept there sometimes. When I asked Miss Melda where Tony slept, she said he went home in the night, but I knew better.

One night Uncle Dudley came home unexpectedly. Miss Melda did not know what to do, because she was expecting Tony that very night. Although Melda worked Uncle Dudley hard, she could not always fool with him. She feared he might use his machete to chop her in his anger. People had been teasing Dudley about his competition, but Uncle Dudley just laughed, and said she couldn't be so mad. Miss Melda did not want him to put two and two together and get four, so to speak.

Miss Melda heard Tony coming up the hill, whistling. She saw Uncle Dudley looking at her, summing her up. If Tony ever knocked on the door, she would be done for. Miss Melda's mind moved fast.

She went to the window and said to Dudley, "Dudley, darling, the night dark eh?" Dudley moved towards the window. Miss Melda grabbed him lovingly, pushed her head through the window and shouted, "Darling it really dark. Lord it dark like, galang back for him deh ya tonight!"

"Yes," said Dudley, after extricating himself from her tight embrace. "It really dark tonight."

Yes, thought Tony as he turned back. *Is a smart way she use to warn me.*

This was what I overheard Miss Melda telling the washerwoman. It hurt me, but if a told Uncle Dudley, what if him kill Miss Melda?

Another time Uncle Dudley came home in the dead of night. He caught Miss Melda off guard. Tony was fast asleep in the bed beside her. Uncle Dudley was inside the house already. She held her breath tight and hoped he would not notice anything, as she huddled up to Tony and pretended to be fast asleep. Luckily for her, Uncle Dudley was drunk. He simply wanted to sleep without disturbing her. He jumped into bed, but as he pulled on the cover, he noticed six feet sticking out. He reasoned to himself that there should be four feet and not six. To make sure, he got off the bed and counted again. This time he got four.

"Oh," he said as he climbed back into bed. "Lately, I find that my eyes have been fooling me." Very soon he was snoring like a woodcutter sawing lumber. Miss Melda cautiously woke Tony and sent him away.

I overheard the washerwoman telling long mouth Liza this. It really hurt me, but if a told Uncle Dudley, a fear for Miss Melda's life.

Dudley
and the Radio

Maas Ernie was migrating, so he gave Uncle Dudley his radio. Uncle Dudley was always saving to buy a radio, but he always ended up using the money. If he did not spend it on drugs, it was spent on rum.

Uncle Dudley was excited. The radio was small but it was loud. Uncle Dudley turned it up to the maximum capacity. All day and all night he played the radio. He loved to listen to the loud music. As soon as he heard talking on one station, he switched to another. Sometimes you could hear him mumbling some of the tunes he heard on the radio. Not even Miss Melda would dare to turn off his radio.

One day Uncle Dudley heard the radio singing *Don't play that song for me.* He could not believe his ears, but as he stared at the radio, the words were repeated – *Don't play it no more.* For the first time since he got the radio, he turned it off.

"Come here Melda!" he called. "You know the man in the radio says I must not play it no more."

Miss Melda laughed. "Dudley, you are too stupid!"

"Is who you calling stupid?" Uncle Dudley sneered at her. "Don't let mi lose mi temper in here today!"

"Mind yuh let people hear yuh say man in radio say yuh musn't play radio no more. They would say yuh lie. They might even send yuh go to mad house, where yuh belong." Miss Melda said the last part of the sentence under her breath, but Uncle Dudley heard and moved menacingly towards her, and threatened to flatten her face.

"All right then!" shouted Miss Melda from a safe distance. "Turn on back the radio and we can see who telling lie."

Uncle Dudley turned the radio on. The loud words boomed *Yuh lie, yuh lie, yuh lie, lie, lie!*

In a blind rage, Uncle Dudley grabbed the radio and smashed it into the wall. The remnants fell to the ground in pieces.

"You idiot!" shouted Miss Melda. "That was just a song that —"

Uncle Dudley moved towards her with fire in his eyes. She ran out of the house and returned one day when he was not there to collect her things.

The Watch Man

Now that Miss Melda was gone, Uncle Dudley lived by himself. The landlord gave him notice, so he went to live in the bush. He continued to cut trees and sold it as lumber. In that way, he could feed himself and his addictive habits.

I felt sorry for Uncle Dudley. At school, children jeered me about my mad uncle. Sometimes when Uncle Dudley left the bush and came on the road, children stoned him and called him Dum Dud.

One day he caught one of them, a fat boy called Elton, and gave him a sound beating. The parents wanted the police to put Uncle Dudley in jail, but they said he acted because he was provoked. They warned the children not to stone Uncle Dudley or provoke him again.

As I have said before, Uncle Dudley was not always mad. Sometimes he acted more sensible than you and I. If you gave him a task and paid him, you could rest assured that it would be properly done.

One day Mr. Lyn, the Chinese shopkeeper, was going away for the weekend. He gave Uncle Dudley fifty dollars and asked him to watch his house. Uncle Dudley positioned himself at the gate. The rain came and he stood at the gate. Night came and he slept at the gate. Nothing could get him away from the gate.

When Mr. Lyn came back, he found Uncle Dudley at the gate.

"What are you doing here?" he asked.

"I am watching your house," said Uncle Dudley.

Poor Uncle Dudley!

Mr. Lyn just shook his head and gave him fifty dollars more.

The Cell Phone

Uncle Dudley got a cell phone. How he came by it, he would not say. I often wondered what he was doing with it for he had no one to call.

Although he was crazy, Uncle Dudley still had an eye for beautiful girls, and there was one in particular that he admired very much.

Pamella worked at the post office. She was an Indian girl with long hair, which she combed in pony tails. Uncle Dudley often saw her when he frequented the post office. It was his custom to visit the post office each day and ask for his mail. While the other workers would chase him away, Pamella always shook her head and smiled. Uncle Dudley grew to like her. She was not as mean as the others.

One day a little piece of paper fell from her bag and Uncle Dudley picked it up, meaning to give it to her. Then he saw her name and some numbers beside it. He knew it was her telephone number. He kept it and as soon as he was safely out of sight, he dialed the number.

"Can't take your call now, but leave your name and number and I will get back to you."

Dudley recognized the voice immediately. He waited until he knew she would be home and dialed the number again.

"Hello," came the voice that sounded like music to his ears.

"How was your day, Pam?" he asked, disguising his voice.

"Fine," she answered. "Who am I speaking with?"

"Wear your beautiful red dress with the rose to work tomorrow," he told her.

"Who is it?" Pamella insisted.

"You are such a sweet lady."

Pamella hung up.

At exactly 9 p.m., the phone rang again.

"Hello Pamella," came the strange voice again.

"Who am I speaking with?" asked Pamella.

"May I come by and keep your company?"

Pamella hung up.

She was becoming concerned. She had heard stories of stalkers and kidnappers. This person seemed to know her whereabouts, and she had not even the slightest notion who he was. She had reason to be afraid for she lived all alone. Alton, her boyfriend, only visited her on weekends, since he worked in the city.

In the morning she would inform the police just to make sure. Luckily there was no more disturbance for the rest of the night.

The next day at work she was very alert, but she saw nobody strange. Uncle Dudley came asking for his mail as usual and the day was uneventful.

Pamella went home after work, cooked and settled down to watch television. At 10 p.m., just as she was about to sleep, the phone rang. She had left a message for Alton to call her so she picked up on the first ring.

"Hello Pamella," came the voice she dreaded. "Want some company?"

"I have company," she lied.

"I know better," retorted the voice at the other end.

She hung up the phone.

The phone rang again and when she answered it was Alton. When she told him about the strange calls, he warned her to be careful.

She reported it to the police the following day. They advised her to take extra safety precautions, which she did. She noticed nothing strange or unusual. However, the calls kept coming.

They came at all hours of the night and the questions became more personal.

"Hi Pamella," he said at 11 p.m. one night. "Are you naked yet?"

She didn't wait to hear more. She just slammed down the phone.

She became a nervous wreck. When Alton visited her that weekend, she clung to him, not wanting him to go. She started making plans to move back to the city. She doubted that the police could protect her, but although she was skeptical, the police were on the case.

One day they saw Uncle Dudley dialing a number. They crept upon him and confiscated the phone. They checked the number he dialed and lo and behold, it was the very same number Pamella had given them.

The phone was confiscated and he was taken to jail. He professed his innocence and demanded that they could not lock him up before he got a phone call. "It is every citizen's right," he said. They allowed him to make the phone call.

Uncle Dudley dialed. At the other end a beautiful Indian girl took up the phone.

"Hello Pamella," came the smooth, familiar voice, she dreaded. "I am going to miss you. They have locked —"

Pamella slammed down the phone.

The Hermit

After Miss Melda left Uncle Dudley, he lived in the bush like a recluse. I feared for his health. He was not eating well and he smoked and drank too much. I often wondered what would happen if he became really ill in the bush. Maybe he would die and decay before anyone found him. However, the people in Walden said the bush was the best place for him.

The only people whom he saw were a few farmers who had their farms near his abode. Sometimes, the dogs followed them to the farm.

One day, Maas Dan-Dan's dog strayed and went to Uncle Dudley's hut. Some leftover food and bones were there, so the dog ate it. After that, the dog visited Uncle Dudley's hut each time Maas Dan-Dan came to the farm.

At first Uncle Dudley did not mind, but when Champy tore up his shirt that he had put out to dry, he became angry. He chased Champy away whenever the dog came to his yard. However, the animal would not take a hint.

"Yuh don't have a yard?" Uncle Dudley asked angrily as he stoned the dog.

He did not have a kitchen. He cooked outside, using three stones to support the pot on the fire. One day Champy turned over the pot with his food and his temper flared. He grabbed his machete and cut off one of the dog's feet.

"Since yuh don't have any yard," he said, "yuh get one now!"

The poor dog managed to totter back to Maas Dan-Dan. When Maas Dan-Dan saw Champy with one foot gone and bleeding profusely, he confronted Uncle Dudley and demanded to know how he was so cruel.

"Cruel?" Uncle Dudley asked incredulously. "I did that dog a favour. He kept pestering me, stealing my food and tearing up my clothes. He did not have any abiding city. He should thank me for giving him a yard."

"And how did you do that?" asked Maas Dan-Dan angrily. He thought it was so useless, arguing with a mad man.

"You fool, three feet makes a yard," said Uncle Dudley before erupting in laughter.

The Verdict

It's amazing how bad news can draw a crowd. It is broad daylight but the crowd is still here.

"A wonder what happen now?" Maas Manto inquires as he is passing to go to his farm.

"Dan-Dan is losing his mind," someone says.

"Yuh want a tell yuh who losing mind!" Maas Dan-Dan shouts. "Oonuh tek oonuh self from mi gate for oonuh adding insult to injury!"

Maas Dan-Dan's gate is wide open. This is odd, because ever since Uncle Dudley cut off one of its feet, Maas Dan-Dan keeps the dog in the yard. The gate is always closed, and a big sign is posted that reads KNOCK BAD DOG. No one dares enter the yard or even go near the gate. Champy is as fierce as a wolf, ready to tear up anyone who even ventures near the gate. The nice stringy mangoes that fall to the ground and rot under the tree testify to the fear Champy invokes in both children and adults.

I look into the yard and see Champy laying in a pool of blood, his head crushed, and a big, bloody rock close by. Someone had used the rock to crush the dog's head.

Maas Dan-Dan is fit to be tied, the way he is angry.

"If I ever catch the coward who kill mi dog is hell and powder house!" he repeats over and over.

If anyone knows who the culprit is, no one is talking. I don't blame them. I wouldn't talk either. I don't like that old dog. He is always barking at people and acting like he would scale the fence and bite them. Moreover I can't forget how he pulled my nice white dress off the line and tore it up, and Maas Dan-Dan refused to replace it, saying it could be any other dog and we must stop picking on his dog.

The excitement is drawing more people to the scene, and among them is Uncle Dudley. Maas Dan-Dan hates him. He has never forgiven him for cutting off the dog's foot. Uncle Dudley approaches and the two men glare at each other.

"Yuh get yuh wish. Champy dead now. Smaddy scale the fence and crush mi dog head. Mi innocent dog!" Maas Dan-Dan says to Uncle Dudley.

"Innocent mi foot!" Uncle Dudley shouts angrily. "That dog is worse than the devil from hell. Nobody can stand him."

"Nobody business fi scale the fence and come in mi yard and kill Champy," Maas Dan-Dan says.

"Mi never scale no fence. Mi climb on the wall and drop the rock on him head," says Uncle Dudley.

A heavy sigh comes from the crowd. How could Uncle Dudley be so stupid as to let Maas Dan-Dan trap him into confessing his crime? Why Uncle Dudley has to be so fool-fool?

Well the people have to hold on to Maas Dan-Dan and Uncle Dudley or there would surely be another death right at the gate.

Maas Dan-Dan reports the crime and Uncle Dudley gets arrested, but everybody puts money together and bails him out.

I don't get to go to the trial, since children can't go inside the courthouse. Papa and Mama go and so I get the full account.

"Dudley get away. Mi so glad. Dudley didn't even have a lawyer to defend him, yet him get away scotch free," Mama says.

Mama relates how Maas Dan Dan told the judge how Uncle Dudley went out of his way to kill his dog, pointing out that it was not the first attempt. He told the judge how Uncle Dudley cut off the dog's foot about a year ago.

"What do you have to say for yourself?" the judge asked Uncle Dudley.

"I'm not guilty. I was doing Maas Dan-Dan a favour, Your Honour."

"Doing me a favour?" asked Maas Dan-Dan incredulously. "Your Honour yuh don't see that this is a mad maniac?"

"Hush up before I charge you for contempt of court!" shouted the judge. "You had your turn to speak. Let the defendant continue."

"Yes Your Honour, I did Maas Dan-Dan a favour," continued Uncle Dudley. "The sign said 'KNOCK BAD DOG', so I knocked the dog, and unfortunately he died."

"That's what the sign read?" the judge asked Maas Dan-Dan.

"Yes Your Honour."

Maas Dan-Dan held up the sign. "See I carry it for evidence. I gave people full warning not to enter my yard or provoke my dog."

The judge examined the sign, scratched his head and hesitated a little before speaking.

"The defendant is not guilty. You are free to go," the judge said.

"This is injustice!" protested Maas Dan-Dan.

The judge glared at him. "The defendant did as you requested. Your dog died because of a comma," he told Maas Dan-Dan.

"The dog was hale and hearty!" protested Maas Dan-Dan. "He was in no coma. He was hit with a rock by this —"

"Order in this court! You omitted a punctuation mark called a comma. The comma should be written after the word knock. Hence the sign would have read KNOCK, BAD DOG. But your sign Sir, said, KNOCK BAD DOG, and that's exactly what the defendant did. The defendant is not guilty."

"But Your Honour!"

"Case dismissed!"

According to Maas Dan-Dan, jackass sey the worl' nuh level, but him should realize that what goes around comes around.

Laughter is the Best Medicine

It has been many years since I left Walden. I got married and migrated to America with my husband. Whenever I come to Jamaica, I visit Uncle Dudley.

He talks pure nonsense. He has really lost his mind. He says I am mad and needs to get my head examined.

I was not comfortable with the idea of his living in the bush by himself, so I built a house for him near the road.

Last year when I visited Jamaica, Uncle Dudley was living in the house. I visited him there. He looked clean and neat. However, he had a terrible pain in his stomach. I took him to see the doctor. He did not want to go, but after tremendous effort and help from the neighbours, I got him to the doctor.

The doctor diagnosed an ulcer stomach and prescribed his medication. He was given a white liquid to be taken twice per day and tablets to be taken every two days. On the first day, I administered the medication myself.

When I visited him the following day, I was surprised to see him out of bed and skipping.

"Uncle Dudley, what are you doing out of bed? You're feeling better already?" I asked.

"That doctor is a mad man!" he said. "Why else would he want a sick man to skip, and every time I skip the pain gets worse!"

"The doctor told you to skip?" I asked.

He showed me the instructions on the box with the tablets. It said, *Take one tablet every other day.*

"There is nothing about skipping," I said.

"When the doctor gave me, he told me that it meant I should take one tablet, skip a day, then take one tablet and so on."

I had to laugh. "Go back to bed Uncle Dudley. You took a tablet yesterday. Don't take any today. Just rest. Tomorrow you take another one. That is what the doctor means. You must take them every other day."

"Oh," he said. "What a stupid fool you chose for a doctor."

What could I do but laugh?

When Two Rams Collide

When Two Rams Collide

Today I am so happy! As I sweep the yard with the broom weed, I keep talking to myself.

Old Frank leave him upstairs house and gone to live with relatives in another parish. Glory to God! Old Frank gone! No more food wrapped up in white kitchen towel to carry to him. No more stairs to climb. No more shouting at the door for him to open it and collect the food. Why they wait so long to tek him? Better late than never though. Glory to God!

Yuh know how long Mama cooking for that old man? Yuh know how I hate carrying food to him? Yuh know how many lies I cook up to wheedle out of taking food to him? Now relatives tek him. Thank God! For years Mama cook for that old man, and she get a little piece of land near bottom yard as compensation. But let mi pop story give yuh.

Shortly after Old Frank vacated his house, a distant relative called Miss Mattie moved in. She took over the house and all of Old Frank's other possessions. I don't like the woman. When Old Frank lived there we could pick tangerine and star apple and search for pears under the pear tree. Now when Miss Mattie sees us picking tangerines she chases us away.

Now she starts farming the land and much to Mama's indignation, she starts moving on to her piece of land, her little legacy from Old Frank. When Mama tells her that Old Frank left the land for her, she laughs in Mama's face.

"Promise is a comfort to a fool," she says. "Old Frank isn't in his right mind. Him promise nuff people what him don't even have. Mi is him close relative, so mi can stake my claim."

"We will see," Mama says. "Time longer than rope."

Unfortunately the argument doesn't stop there. The piece of land is the focal point of contention.

Miss Mattie's husband returns from England. He is a thin, wiry man named Maas Zeke. To me, Maas Zeke makes England look bad. People returning from abroad are supposed to look good, but he lost a screw in England. His oversized pants have loops, but he does not push his belt through them. Instead he pushes his shirt into his pants which are drawn up way above his waist, and then he ties the belt around it, creating plenty gathers at the waist. He moves with the odd grace of a disjointed robot on an urgent mission. He has a dry cough which he can't get rid of and that is attributed to the cold in England.

With Maas Zeke to back her, Miss Mattie becomes very bold. Although Papa builds a fence to mark the border of Mama's land, she tears off a piece of the fence and ties her goat on Mama's premises. Papa unties the goat and yokes it to a tree on their side of the fence. The following day the goat is back on Mama's land. On seeing this, Papa again moves the goat, but instead of tying it back to a tree, he lets it loose and bawls for Miss Mattie and Maas Zeke. He stands with one hand on his hip and his machete in the other, waiting.

The swift mechanical steps approach, signalling the arrival of Maas Zeke.

"Morning Lanzo," he says.

Papa does not return his greeting. "Tie that goat over here again, an' yuh gwine eat curry goat till yuh cloy," Papa hisses at him.

While Miss Mattie chases and catches the goat, Maas Zeke and Papa get into a heated argument. Miss Mattie quickly ties the goat and joins them.

"Yuh witchcraft yuh!" Papa bawls at her. "Mi wife get the little legacy an' yuh red yeye can't resist it!"

"How dare you call Mattie witchcraft!" croaks Maas Zeke. "Yuh want to eat those word in the court of laws? I will bring yuh up for malicious slander yuh know bwoy!"

Papa leers at him.

"Yuh calling mi witchcraft," Miss Mattie says. "Yuh ever buck mi up when yuh go a any a yuh obeah man dem?"

Papa's reply shocks us.

"Yes Matilda!" Papa shouts. "Mi meet yuh there Matilda! Mi meet yuh there a look promotion!"

Explosive laughter erupts from the curious crowd that has converged on the scene to listen.

In a bid to defend his wife's honour, Maas Zeke doubles his fists and advances toward Papa. Papa starts hacking down the limb of a tree, while we wonder for what purpose.

He trims the leaves from the limb and shouts, "Come Zeke bwoy, mek a give yuh a beating!"

A fearful look creeps onto Maas Zeke's face, and he takes a step backward.

Hear Miss Mattie to Maas Zeke, as she pushes him, "Go up to him Zeke! Lanzo ah bwoy to yuh! Him can't lick yuh! Go up to him!"

At this point Bull and Bobby hold on to Papa.

I am horrified to see Miss Mattie pushing her little frail husband into the direct path of deadly danger. If my two brothers fail to restrain Papa, there might be tragedy today.

The little crowd that gathers manages to pacify Papa and shield Maas Zeke.

From that day they avoid each other. If Maas Zeke sees Papa on one side of the road, he walks on the other side. It is a similar situation with Mama and Miss Mattie. They deliberately ignore each other.

Now we get news that Old Frank passed away in his sleep. One week later a little crowd gathers at the shop and a brown lady in spectacles reads the will. Much to Mama's delight and Miss Mattie's disappointment, the piece of land was indeed willed to Mama as compensation for cooking for Old Frank.

I am very relieved, because this has put an end to the enmity between my parents and that odd couple. Now they are friendly towards each other again.

Thank God!

The
Ackee
Tree

The Ackee Tree

Our property has a lot of land space. There is a big yard to sweep and there is also a coffee walk, which is also a banana walk, which deposits trash and all sorts of rubbish into the yard, creating more work for people like me, who have to sweep the yard every day.

Towards the back of the coffee walk is a big ackee tree. Its trunk is very wide and the branches spread high above the banana and coffee trees. It just stands in the coffee walk like a great white elephant, failing to bear any fruit year after year. Mama says that as long as she can remember it has been there, but not an ackee will it surrender.

My brother often uses this tree to trap birds. Alton climbs the tree and makes what he calls a choky. He uses cord to make a noose, which he ties to a high limb of the tree. He then puts a very ripe tangerine in front of the noose. The trick is that the bird, in order to peck the tangerine, has to push its head through the noose. When the bird's head is in the noose, Alton draws a cord that is suspended to the ground. If he is swift enough, the victim is caught when the noose tightens. This requires a lot of time and patience, and sometimes he is under the tree for hours without catching a single bird.

Sometimes, he makes a calaban, which he places under the tree. This is another trap to catch the birds. He uses sticks, which are neatly arranged and tied to make a little house. One can see between the spaces what is inside the house. An orange is placed under the calaban. A slender stick is then used to prop up the calaban, so that the bird can go in to eat the orange. As soon as the bird bounces on the calaban, the stick falls and it is trapped.

I often wonder why he bothers. Once in a blue moon he manages to catch a teeny bird. He cleans it up and roasts it and it tastes bitter as gall. Anyway, when Papa decides to chop down the tree, Alton begs him not to, because he wants to continue his bird-catching in the ackee tree. Papa grants him his wish.

"Just for one more year," Papa says. "If that tree don't bear this year, a chopping it down. It preventing the coffee trees from getting sunlight and bearing more coffee beans."

Well, today when I look up into the ackee tree I see blossoms. I am excited.

"Mama, the ackee tree blossoming!" I tell Mama.

"Let's hope it bears this time," Mama says. "Its life depends on it."

Then wonder of wonders, the ackee tree bears ackees!

"What no happen in a year happen in a day!" Mama says, and I can see that she is glad.

We watch the fruits progress from tiny green pods to brilliant red fruits. Then we wait for them to open and display their black eyes. No such luck.

"Mama, why the ackees won't open so we can eat ackee and salt fish?" I ask.

"Give them time," Mama chides. "Yuh can't rush God's handiwork."

But a lot of time has passed. Every day I look up at the big bunches of brilliant red, but there are no black eyes looking back at me.

Today, Miss Emma visits us. She is Uncle Tiger's wife, but we still call her Miss Emma instead of Aunt Emma. She is a plump, pleasant woman, whose body often shakes with laughter. I proudly show her the ackee tree laden with fruits.

"The sad thing is that they won't open," I tell her.

"They look fit and big enough to burst," says Miss Emma. "Is full time they pop now. If yuh want them to open, yuh don't know that yuh must go under the tree and laugh?"

"Go under the tree and laugh!" I exclaim.

Instead of answering, Miss Emma drags all of us under the tree, even Papa. We all look up into the tree and laugh. I feel so silly. I don't believe a word that she says, but I find myself laughing at how silly we all look, laughing up into the ackee tree. I glance at Miss Emma, whose body is shaking vigorously as she throws back her head and laughs the loudest. Now we are laughing till tears are streaming down some of our faces.

"Come from under the tree!" Papa brings us back to our senses. "This is all foolishness! Miss Emma where yuh get this nonsense from?"

"Doubtful Thomas!" she jeers as we go back into the yard.

The next day I am the first to see the shiny black eyes peeping out of the red pods. I am so elated!

"Mama the ackees opening!" I shout.

Mama comes running out and counts six opened ackees. We laugh under the tree again. By noon, some more ackees burst wide open. We laugh again and by evening all we can see are brilliant black eyes peeping from the red ackee pods in the tree.

Alton picks the ackees and Mama cooks ackee and salt fish and dumplings, and yellow yam and St. Vincent yam for dinner.

What a feast we have, man!

Miss Emma can't stop talking about it. She is so surprised that we did not know that we should laugh under the tree to make the ackees pop! Papa says she is talking pure nonsense and Alton says it is just coincidence.

But they can always talk. I love ackee and salt fish so till!

And yuh si now that I know what I know?

Every day till ackee season done, I going under that ackee tree to laugh!